MW01422932

CANDY ISLAND
-A sweet-
Getaway
Milkshake museum
CANDY CANYON
Peanut Butter pass
sweet sanctuar

Slushie Slopes

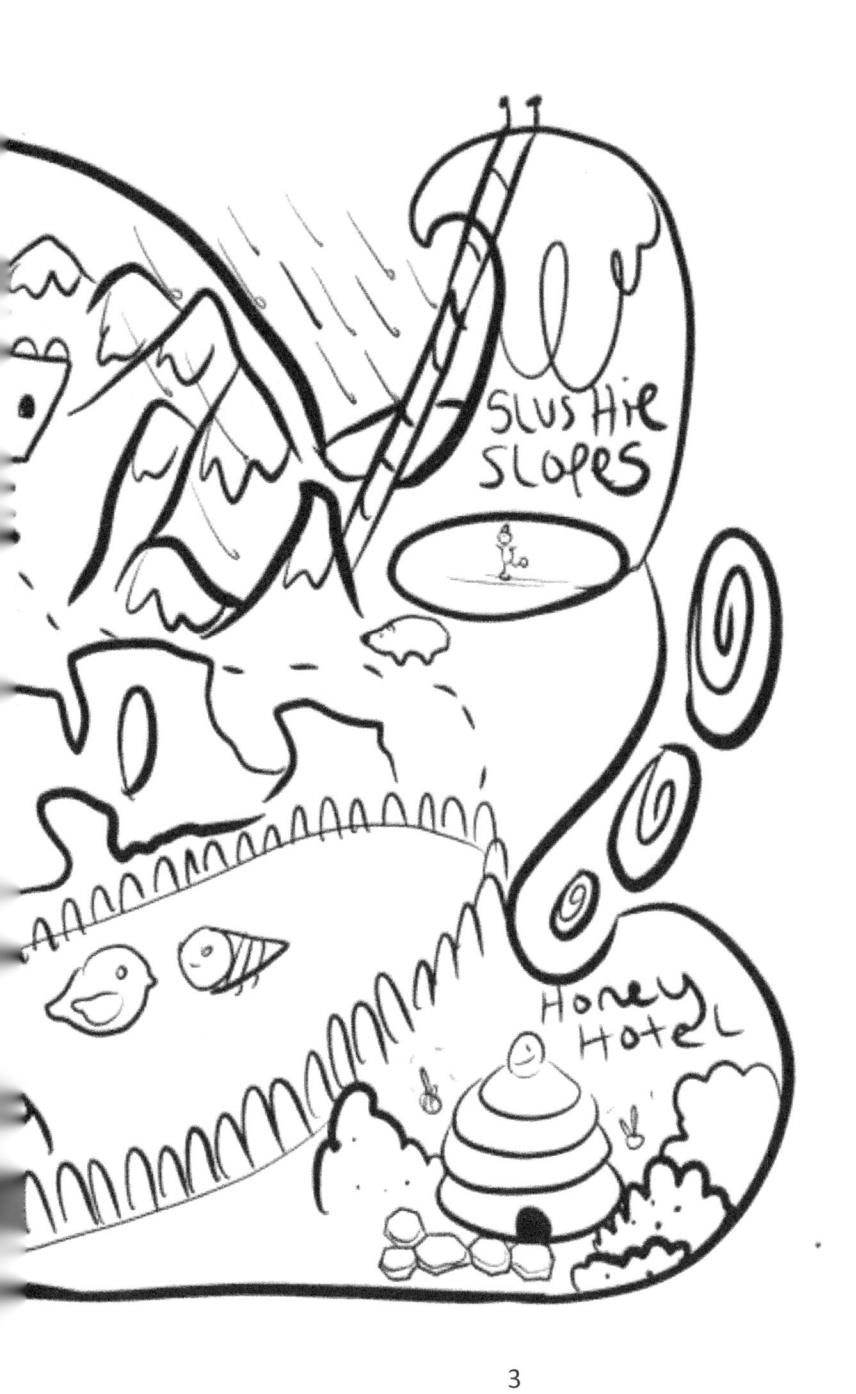

Honey Hotel

Odd Lands

Book Five

A Sweet Getaway

Written and illustrated by

Nicole Kaczmarek

Odd Lands
A Sweet Getaway
Book Five
Copyright © 2020
All rights reserved.
Text copyright by Nicole Kaczmarek
Illustrations and cover art by Nicole Kaczmarek—Done in Procreate.
No part of this publication may be reproduced, stored in a retrieval system, or transmitted, in any form or by any means, (electronic, mechanical, photocopying, recording or otherwise), without prior written permission from the author.

This book is a work of fiction. Names, characters, places, and incidents are either the product of the author's imagination or are used fictitiously, and any resemblance to actual persons, living or dead, business establishments, events or locales is entirely coincidental.
Questions contact, nicolekaczmarek93@gmail.com
ISBN 9798577170745
Published in the United States: KDP

Contents

1. Together — 9
2. A lift to Candy Island — 17
3. Peanut Butter Pass — 31
4. Candy Canyon — 37
5. Milkshake Museum — 43
6. Jen and the Gems — 49
7. Slushie Slopes — 53
8. Candy Thieves — 63
9. Sweet Sanctuary — 69
10. Honey hotel — 75

1.

<u>Together</u>

At home, Todd stood out back beneath the porch light and played fetch with Flint.
Grrrrrrr.
Flint bopped his squeaky toy beneath the deck and refused to fetch it.
"What's the problem?" Todd asked.
He took out his phone to use as a flashlight and climbed over the railing. Todd crawled on his belly through the tight dusty space beneath deck and grabbed the toy, but a red glow further in caught his eye. Flint continued to race around and began barking up a storm.
"Here, take your toy and go," Todd threw out the squeaky toy and grabbed the glowing object.
"Another gem…Hm…" Todd twirled the shiny red piece between his fingers and studied the metal casing it was in.

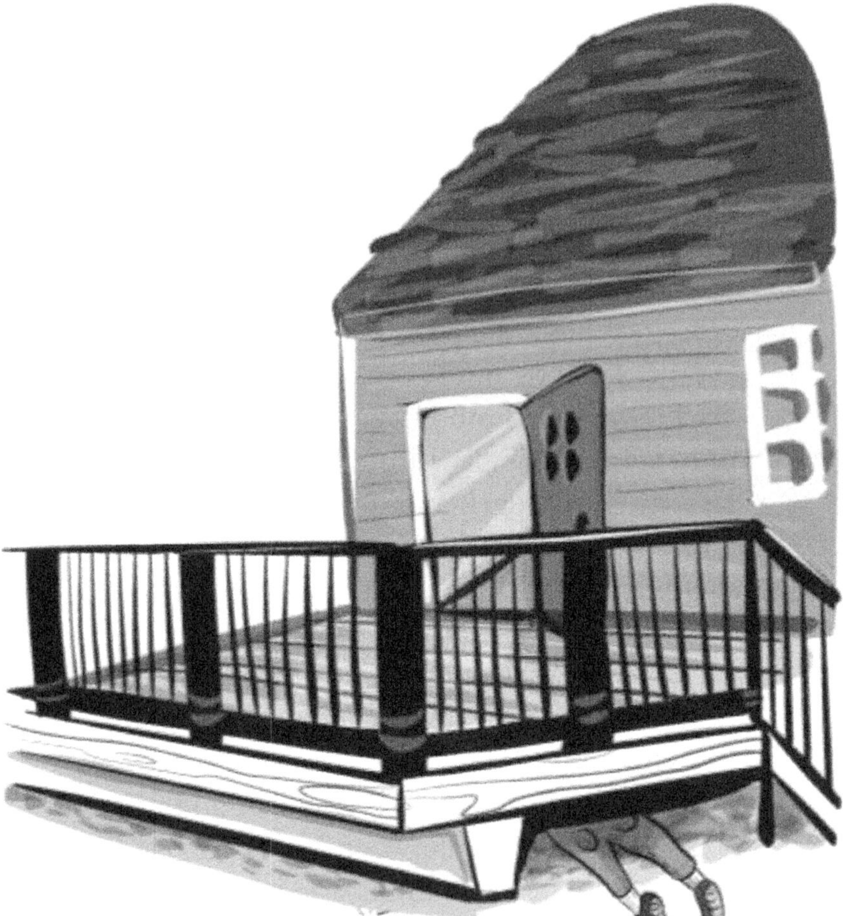

"Jeez, calm down," Todd said crawling out backwards while Flint continued to bark.

Placing more pressure on his arms, Todd gripped the gem tighter which caused a laser blast to shoot from the gem up through the deck—Two more blasts followed.

"Woah!"

"Todd?" Anastasia came outside and noticed smoke rising from holes in the planks.

"Get back! Watch out! This thing's dangerous!" Todd exclaimed.

He shimmied out from under the deck, dropped the gem in the grass and ran up by Anastasia.

"What are you two doing? It's cold out here," Anastasia said and pulled a blanket over her shoulders.

"That thing's a freaking laser! Have you talked to your mom about any of these gems?" Todd asked.

"Laser? No. She's not too open about any of the gem stuff," Anastasia told him and picked up Flint.

"Oh, hey you two. Dinners almost ready," Jen strolled out.

She galloped down the steps and stopped before the red glowing gem in the grass.

"Whew...Thought I'd lost this," Jen said. She swiftly stuck the gem in her coat pocket and headed to the garage.

"What the heck's all the ruckus out here, boy?" Grandpa came to the back door after hearing Todd yell.

"Nothing, we were just coming in," Anastasia told him.

The smell of thanksgiving dinner filled the house, and for first time in a long while, the dining room table was full. Laughter flowed till night, and in a way, everything felt right.

"What a fantastic evening. Thanks again for all the help, Jen. Now for my favorite part," Grandpa said and reached for dessert. While cutting the pie an idea struck him.

"You know...I've had quite a sweet tooth lately. What do you all think about a vacation?" Grandpa suggested.

Everybody paused.

"But, Grandpa, what about your leg?" Todd looked to his cane.

The thought of adventuring like old times took over Grandpa's thoughts, teasing of what fun could be had once again. It had been years since he had traveled out of town.

"Don't think about it too much, boy," Grandpa said quick and nervously awaited their response.

"Where'd you have in mind?" Jen asked.

Grandpa smiled, left his pie, and went into the back room looking for a special map.

Slap.

He came back and palmed a frosting-stained paper down on the kitchen table.

"Candy Island…A sweet getaway," Grandpa said. Flint licked up a sprinkle that rolled out onto the table.

Anastasia sat back and watched Grandpa and her mom giggle over the map like they were kids again.

"I hear they have quite a stash of gold too," Grandpa winked at Todd.

"And the rainbow gem…If pirates haven't snatched it, Jen thought to herself.

"So, we'll go?" Grandpa checked.

Todd shook his head, yes.

"For adventure!" Grandpa shouted and held his glass in the air.

Everyone clanked their cups and celebrated the night away.

2.
A Lift to Candy Island

    Flint raced through the sand while Todd sat at the dock and stared out at the empty sea. He'd thought a lot about his boat since it had disappeared, and even more he wondered how they would travel anywhere without it. The fate of the family fishing business hung heavy on his shoulders and a silly old kayak wasn't going to do anything. Why Grandpa wanted to take a vacation when they were in such rough shape boggled Todd's mind.
    "Guess what I've got," Grandpa came behind Todd waving papers.
    "Plane tickets…Where'd you get these?" Todd asked and read the destination. *Sebenion Mountains.*
    "Spent all night figuring out that online internet purchasing, so I guess you could say I'm an official PC whiz now," Grandpa bragged.
    "You can land by plane at Candy Island?" Todd asked.

"No, but it's the closest landing point…I'll get us there, don't worry, boy," Grandpa stuffed the tickets in his pocket.

"That should be interesting…" Todd said and whistled for Flint.

Anastasia overheard and came onto the dock.

"Is there anything specific we'll need to pack?" she asked.

"Just ready a light bag…Only thing I need is my plans," Grandpa patted something in his pant pocket.

"Oh, but maybe bring plenty of water, sugar will make ya thirsty," Grandpa added.

"We leave tomorrow!" Grandpa excitedly shook Todd and Anastasia's shoulder.

The following morning, Jen was up before sunrise and ready to go. She sat on her piled up suitcases and sipped coffee while everyone else woke.

"Where's your bags?" Jen asked Anastasia who came out with only her backpack.

"I'm not trying to carry my whole wardrobe around, Mom," Anastasia said.

Todd threw on his backpack as well and went to find Grandpa who seemed to be missing.

"Grandpa!" Todd called outside. He'd looked everywhere and if they were going to make their flight, they needed to leave in the next five minutes.

Toot-toot...

Todd's jaw dropped as Grandpa cruised up the driveway in a baby blue electric scooter.

"Oh my gosh Arthur," Jen laughed.

"If I want to keep up out there, I've got to have something," Grandpa laughed along.

"Taxi's here!" Anastasia said and helped load everything into the van.

"Step on it!" Grandpa told the driver.

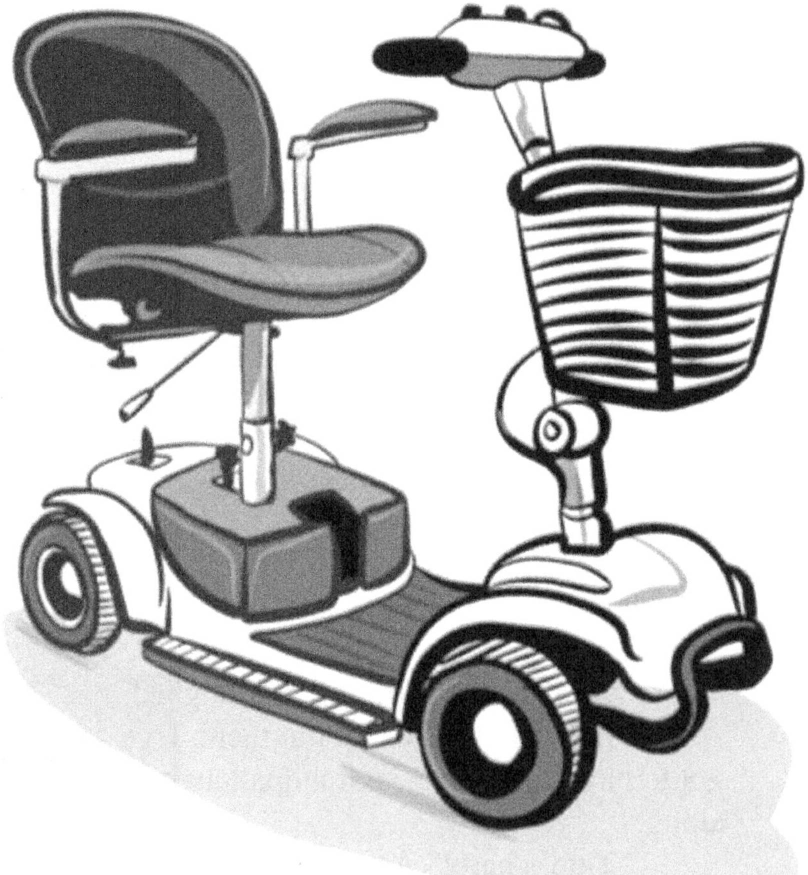

Arrival at the airport was chaotic. Sounds echoed back and forth while footsteps stampeded the gates. Flint whimpered all the way through security while in his carrying cage.

"It's only for a couple of hours, Flint," Anastasia patted his nose through the cage and loaded him onto the cargo cart.

"Sad to hear him cry like that…" Todd said as they walked off.

"Yeah, he plays tough but he's just a small baby inside," Anastasia said.

The four of them tried to stay together through the crowds, but it was difficult with everyone pressed shoulder to shoulder.

"Last call for flight zero-four-one-five…" an attendant said over the airport speaker.

"That's us! Five more doors up…" Todd pointed.

"C'mon speed it up," Jen said.

Everyone started to speed walk, but Grandpa came racing in for the win on his scooter going five miles per hour.

Out of breath everyone boarded the plane and were finally seated.

"All there is left to do is relax and enjoy the view," Grandpa leaned back and glanced out the window.

Anastasia looked at a photo of Flint on her phone and hoped he wasn't too scared back in the cargo.

As the plane took off tilted towards the sky, Todd closed his eyes and tried to remember his time on top of the mountain, that being up high wasn't always bad.

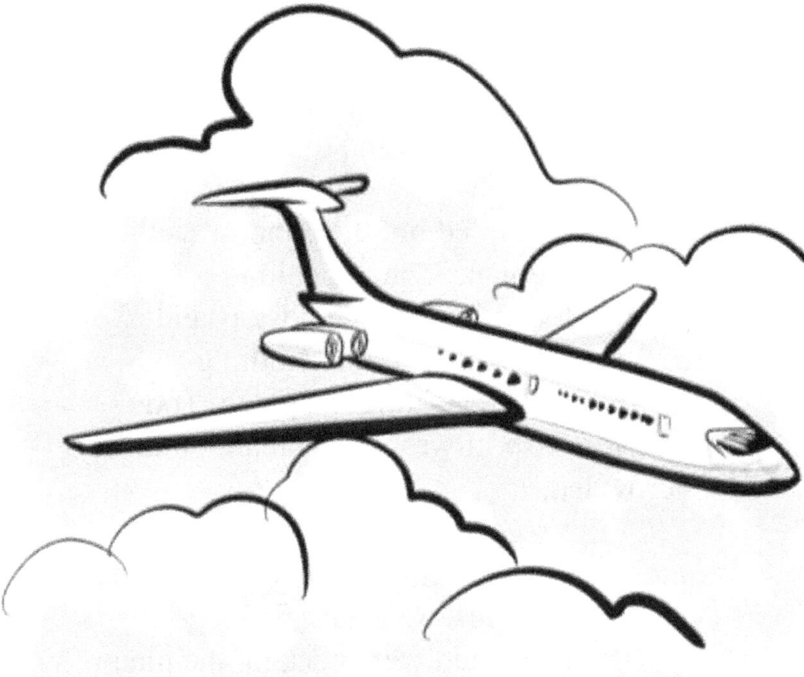

"Brace yourselves for landing in ten…" the pilot said over the speaker.

In the cargo area, Flint was tired from nipping and scratching at the lock. Descending to land, the plane hit a rough patch in the wind and bashed Flint's cage against the wall. The door popped open just enough for Flint to squeeze out and he was free. He sniffed the air and took off through an open vent.

Todd gleamed out the window as the plane soared down. The Sebenion Mountains looked to be a woodsy island filled with rocks and rivers—Nothing candyish in sight. Exiting the plane, Todd noticed this airport was much smaller and less crowded.

"Flint's gone!" Anastasia came running in a panic with his empty cage.

"He can't just be gone…Let's go look," Todd said and went back on the plane with her to search.

In the meantime, Grandpa rode his scooter out to the docks with Jen looking for an available sailor. No fairies or businesses would be up for this kind of task, they had to find someone who could spare some time and be willing to trust a stranger.

"See anything?" Jen asked looking over all the boats at the dock.

"Hard to say…They all seem pretty busy…Follow me…" Grandpa rode off.

"Excuse me, ever heard of Candy Island?" Grandpa asked a woman who was unloading barrels from a boat. She had grey tinted teeth, her hair was stuffed into a hat and she smelled of fish slime.

"Candy? It ain't Halloween," the sailor laughed.

"All jokes aside, just looking for a lift," Grandpa held his map open.

"Sure, I've heard these tales, but never seen any proof," she said side eyeing the map.

"Well, I'm willing to pay what I've got if you'd take us one way," Grandpa said and pulled out his wallet.

"Aye…I'd rather have those fancy suitcases there," the sailor pointed to Jens luggage.

"Fine…Just let me take out my sweater at least," Jen huffed and handed over her designer suitcases.

"Names Gretch…Come on and hop aboard," the sailor said.

Bark! Bark!

Flint came racing towards Grandpa and hopped onto his lap.

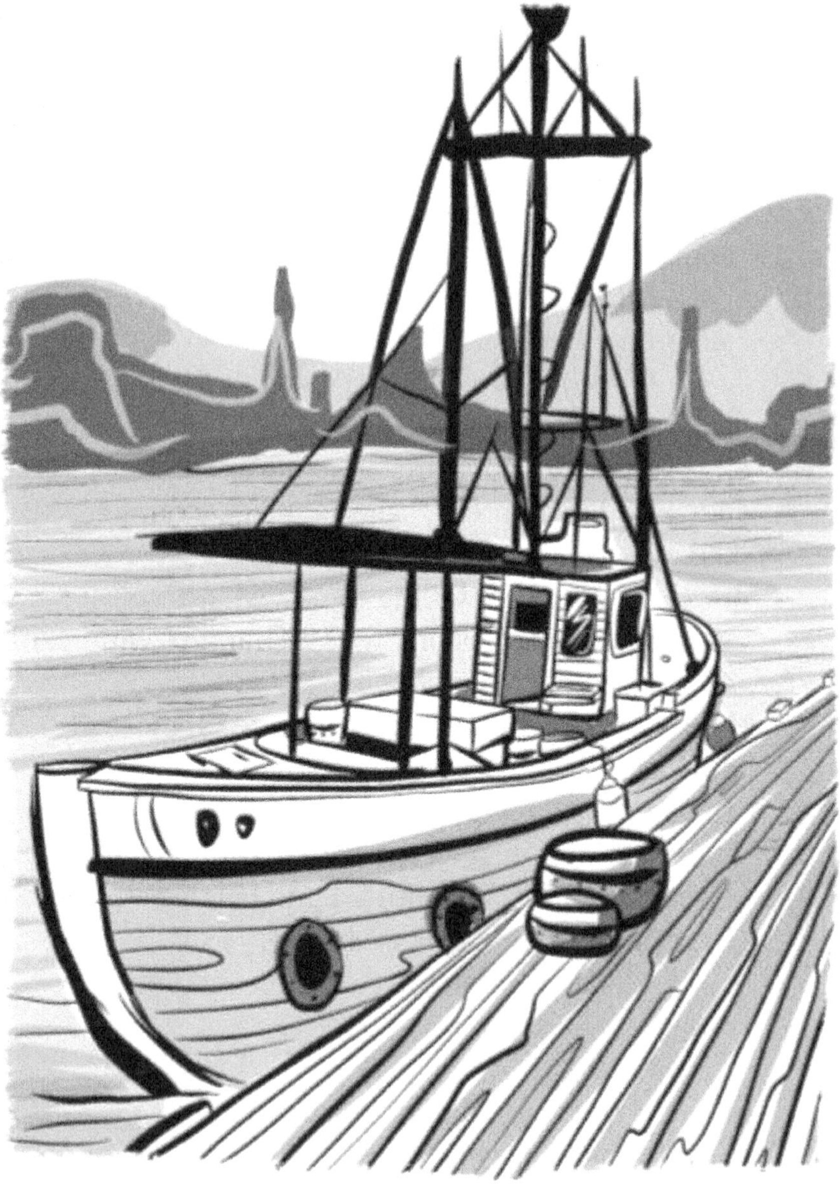

"That's a relief...I'll go get them," Jen patted Flint's head and went to find Todd and Anastasia.

"Hope you don't mind a couple more passengers," Grandpa mentioned.

Sharing no reply, Gretch continued to work with a sour face. As much as Grandpa disliked the chance of the maps, locations, or his family's safety landing in the wrong hands, this felt like his one and only option.

"There you are!" Anastasia raced over and scooped up her furry friend.

"Okay..." Todd squinted at the patchy boat that seemed as though it hadn't been cleaned like, ever—You can tell a lot about someone from their boat.

"Did you plan this part of the trip on the internet too?" Todd whispered to Grandpa.

"Boy, let me tell you about the time I parachuted from a cliff and accidentally landed smack dab on the tallest pile in the city dump. It was awful, I probably smelled like horrendous zombie armpits from a mile away, but I got through and still made it to my destination...You know, it worked out," Grandpa shrugged.

"Right," Todd nodded.

Below deck there had to be but four feet from floor to ceiling. Jen shuffled to the bathroom and opened the rusty door only to find a man passed out on the floor.

"Eh, that's me crew, Wendle, but no mind…We don't have locks or many hecks given on this vessel," Gretch laughed and grabbed a drink from the mini fridge.

"Great…" Jen cringed.

They set off without much enthusiasm, Gretch was a serious sailor who seemed to keep conversation to a minimum.

At sea, Todd sat at the bow with his spyglass and searched for anything out of the ordinary. It was only an estimated three-hour sail, but he hadn't seen a thing besides water.

"I hope it exists," Todd looked to Grandpa who was staring out into the sky.

3.

Peanut Butter Pass

"Land!" Gretch called out and steered passed between a series of large rocks towards shore.

"Aye, this is as far as I go…Too many odd rocks here that could do damage," Gretch said looking confused as to why they were a bright pink color.

Gretch had Wendle extend a wide splintered plank to the beach and Jen was the first one off, but once her feet hit the sandy shore she was stopped in her tracks. The beach was so sticky that hundreds of shoes stayed stuck upon its sugary surface.

"All these shoes look like a warning…" Anastasia commented and advised everyone to take theirs off.

"It's stuck like glue!" Gretch tried to pull the plank back in but it wouldn't budge.

"Whatever. I've got all I need. Good luck!" Gretch said. She scribbled down the coordinates to the island, snatched a bundle of lollie-flowers growing in the water and sailed off.

Grandpa rode his scooter on the beach, but it was moving no quicker than a snail.

"The map says we should pass through a village...That is, if we can make it off this sand before sunset," Todd said watching everyone struggle to walk.

An hour later they'd made it across the beach when,

Boop...

The battery on Grandpa's scooter was running out.

"Well, I didn't anticipate that to happen so fast, but oh well. I've got another," he said and plugged in a spare.

"What's that standing there?" Anastasia asked.

In the distance, Jen could see a tall chocolaty statue blocking the bridge to cross peanut butter pond. They approached the bridge and were halted by a sleeping warrior.

"As guardian of the candies, you may not pass..." the peanut butter cup warrior stood and held their stance.

Todd tried to explain, "But we..."

"As guardian of the candies, you may not pass..." the peanut butter cup warrior repeated.

Jen started to sneak past, but as she did the candy statues large torso spun like a sharp chocolate saw. They held out their wooden sword and transformed into a weapon of doom. Without hesitation, Jen took out her wand of time and froze the chocolate warrior where they stood.

"Wha—I didn't know you had gems, Jen! You should know better by now. Those things aren't meant for human hands," Grandpa yelled. He was infuriated.

"If I don't take them, I'm sure someone else will," Jen said and slid the wand back into her coat pocket.

"I don't have time for your shenanigans anymore…Forget it," Grandpa said and rode off on his scooter.

"How else were you going to get by? A thanks would be fine!" Jen yelled and unfroze the warrior before following.

34

On the other side of the bridge was a few gingerbread houses, but all was quiet. Pieces of candy slowly floated across the thick peanut butter pond, and the ground was still a little sticky causing Grandpa to fall behind. Beginning to think this was all a bad idea Todd went to help him along.

"Is there anything I can do?" Todd asked.

"I'm fine, boy…Thanks. Life feels like a race, but we've all got different engines and there's no real finish line, so long as you've got a smiling heart you're winning," Grandpa said beside him.

Todd smiled.

4.

Candy Canyon

The rocks beside the path started to stretch taller and taller as they neared the canyons.
"Do you hear singing?" Jen asked and noticed the trees and ground starting to shake.
Crack!
One of the trees broke from the ground and rose singing,
"Laaaaaaaaaa!"
"Ah, jellybean trees...When they sing that's how you know they're ripe," Grandpa said and picked a green one off the ground.
"Woah...Hold on..." Todd stopped before a change of yellow ground. Ahead, every single thing was yellow, even the sky.
"What is this, some kind of trick?" Anastasia tapped her foot on the yellow dirt—It was fine.
"Should be a short stroll...Don't worry, we won't turn yellow, but we'll sure stick out so keep moving," Grandpa said and scooted on.

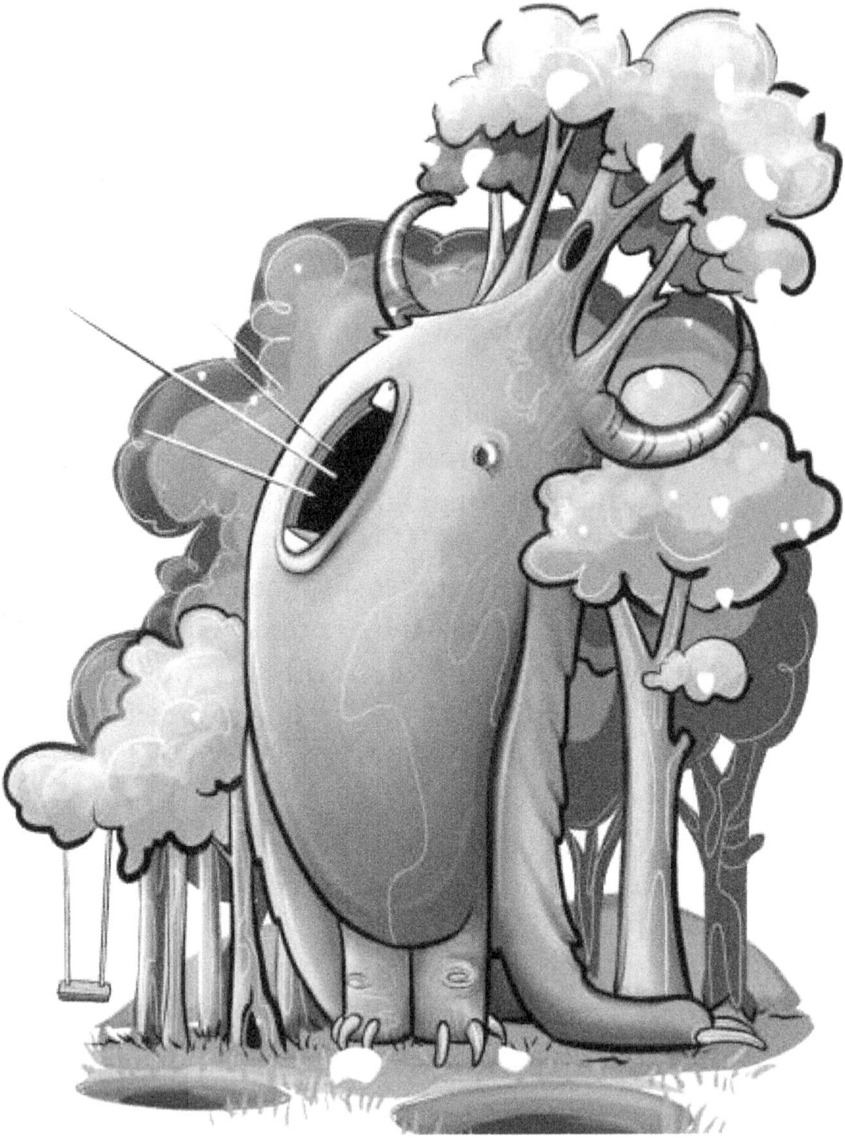

Todd gawked at a split in half house furnished with of course nothing but yellow and more yellow.

"Hey! What are you looking at?" a creature in the bathroom yelled at Todd. All the creatures looked the same, like rabbit-turtles.

Anastasia rubbed her eyes, "This place is messing with my head."

While crossing the street a passing creature was babbling loudly into a banana. "Man...Whateva...I've got groceries on the poodle, the mouse just knocked over the new sofa and the twins are rolling each other up in the rug like some kinda cloth burritos...And don't even get me started on the toothpicks," the yellow creature went on.

"Not sure, if I want to hang around here much longer," Jen said beginning to feel uncomfortable as more creatures crowded the street.

"Almost there," Grandpa remained calm.

"Yeah, see there's some people here...What do ya want me ta do?" another creature whispered into a banana and looked Todd up and down.

Bump

"Sorry..." Todd apologized for bumping shoulders with one of the creatures.

"Man...Whateva..." they snapped their fingers in his face before moving along.

"The exit! No more yellow!" Anastasia spotted normalcy and raced to the end of the canyon.

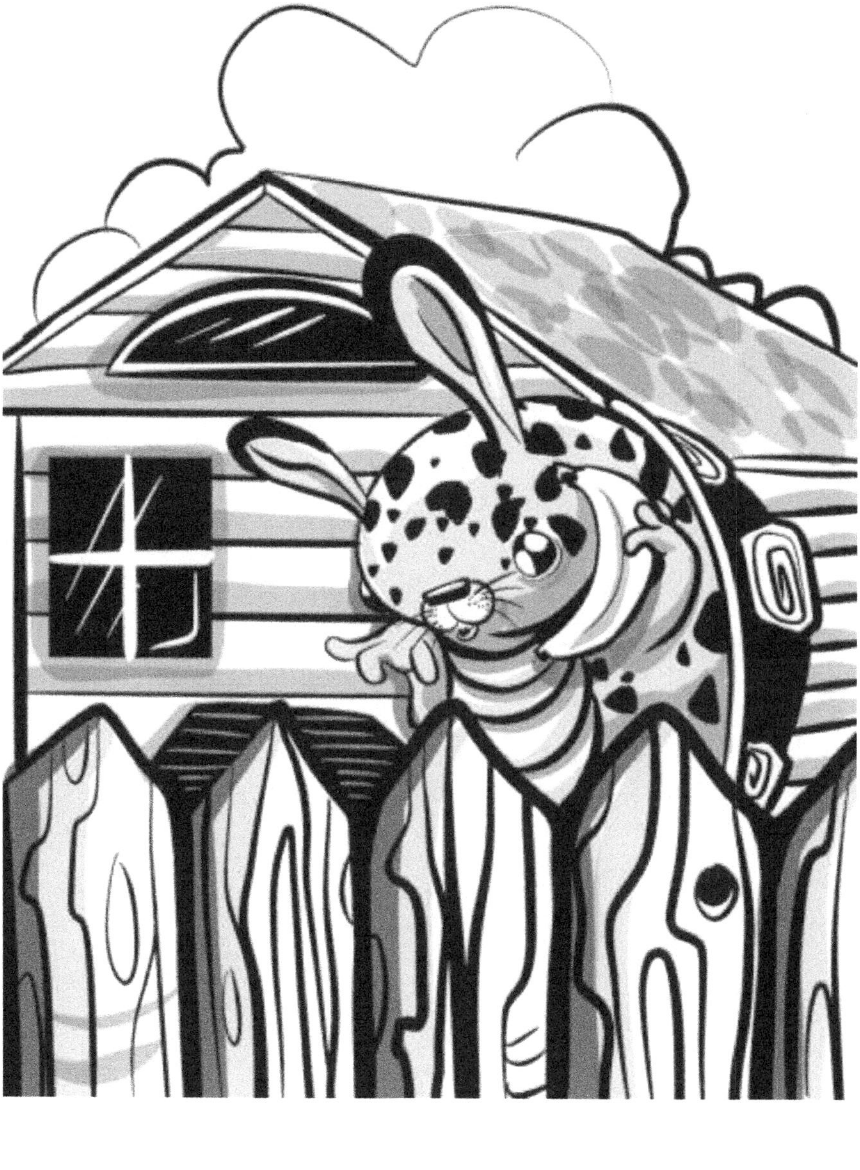

5.

Milkshake Museum

"A Museum about milkshakes. Do you think it's even worth going in here?" Todd asked and read over the map.

"It's a museum boy, when you go on vacation, you tour," Grandpa said and rode through the doors.

"And I could go for a milkshake," Jen added.

"Oh, these islands are always a tour, that's for sure," Todd said and watched a peppermint bird land above the glass-stacked doorway.

Inside, they were directed between red velvet roping to the main room where a sign read,

The tour starts here…

Everything in the museum was pristine, informative, and sweet.

"Welcome to the Milkshake Museum! My name is Rory," said a man in a black suit.

"And I'm Moka," said a cat beside him.

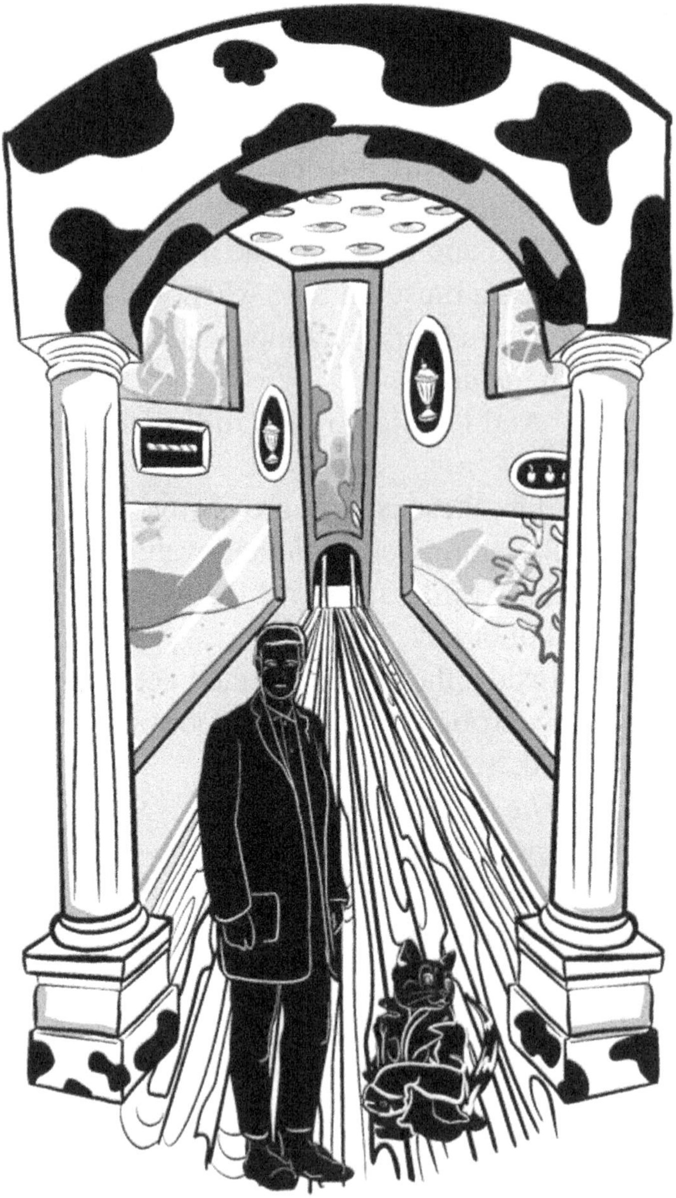

"A talking cat—I'm not surprised," Jen commented.

Flint glared at the brown cat who was wearing a baggy trench coat and standing on its hind legs.

"Remember me from the mountain?" Grandpa stood from his scooter to shake Rory's hand.

"Oh, wow, has it been a while! We still have your photo up in the library from when you saved the cows from that avalanche," Rory said proud.

"Well, it's good to be back. How about a tour for these here kids?" Grandpa suggested.

"Absolutely," Rory clapped twice and an owl in the form of a book flapped down and landed belly up in his hands.

"These owls keep record of every milkshake recipe there is. What's your favorite?" Rory asked.

"Do you have any lactose free kinds?" Jen asked.

"Sure, we've got it all; almond, cow, coconut, goat, rice, soy, oat, cashew, you name it," Rory went on and walked them to a wall of dispensers. It was a buffet of ice cream.

"Fill a cup for the walk," Rory said with a mouth full of whipped cream.

Milkshakes in hand they walked the silent halls that held moments of time as if they were today. Jen stopped at a black and white photo of Rory and Grandpa holding pickaxes at Candy Mountain, and they had the rainbow gem.

"Hmm…" she squinted.

"To the left you'll see the tallest tower from the nineteen-fifty-five glass stacking competition…Still standing strong," Rory said and pinged one of the glasses.

While on the tour, Todd couldn't help but notice that every hallway had an aquarium built into the wall and even in some ceilings. Anastasia pressed her face to the glass and watched a candy fish squiggle by.

"Why so many aquariums?" Anastasia asked.

"It's magnificent right…The way two worlds can merge," Rory smiled and looked up to see a passing gargantuan gummy goldfish.

"Well, c'mon, more to see," Rory said and led them through the library.

Flint had been curiously following the walking cat until he accidentally stepped on Moka's trench coat causing them both to tumble over.

Bat…Bat…

"Back off a bit!" Moka batted at Flint's nose.

"In this room, we display all the straw sculptures…Our most famous one being the red cherry made from two-hundred-fifty-thousand and-seventy-seven straws to be exact," Rory read from a plaque.

"What about the kitchen where all the magic happens," Grandpa asked.

"Half of its boarded up right now, I've got workers coming, but business has been behind due to some pesky snowmen breaking in and devouring all of my ingredients," Rory stressed.

"Ah, ha, it's always something…Well how about the old diner, is that still running?" Grandpa asked.

"Great idea. It's actually been remodeled since you've been here too. Come see," Rory directed the way.

Listening to music in the diner, Todd and Anastasia finished their shakes and talked of crazy concoctions while Grandpa and Rory talked privately in the booth.

Moka stared Flint down as he snuck behind candy jars on the counter.

Hiss…

"I think this wraps up our tour," Rory told everyone.

6.

Jen and the Gems

"So long, thanks for everything!" Grandpa waved goodbye.

On their way to the mountains, the path had broken clean off to a drop with a detour sign pointing down.

"Uh, how's that a detour?" Grandpa asked a nearby construction ice cream.

"Lava cake erupted and took out half the path so we're fixing it up best we can. But, if you need a ride down, I'd be happy to help," the ice cream said.

"Is that an oversized cupcake wrapper?" Todd asked.

"Promise it's the gentlest way or else you'll have to go back and all the way around," the ice cream said.

"You might need a double wrapper though, just incase…" the ice cream said to Grandpa after seeing his hefty scooter.

Todd went first, he stepped through the wrapper door and tried not to think about the far drop. The ice cream turned on a fan and sent the wrapper flying.

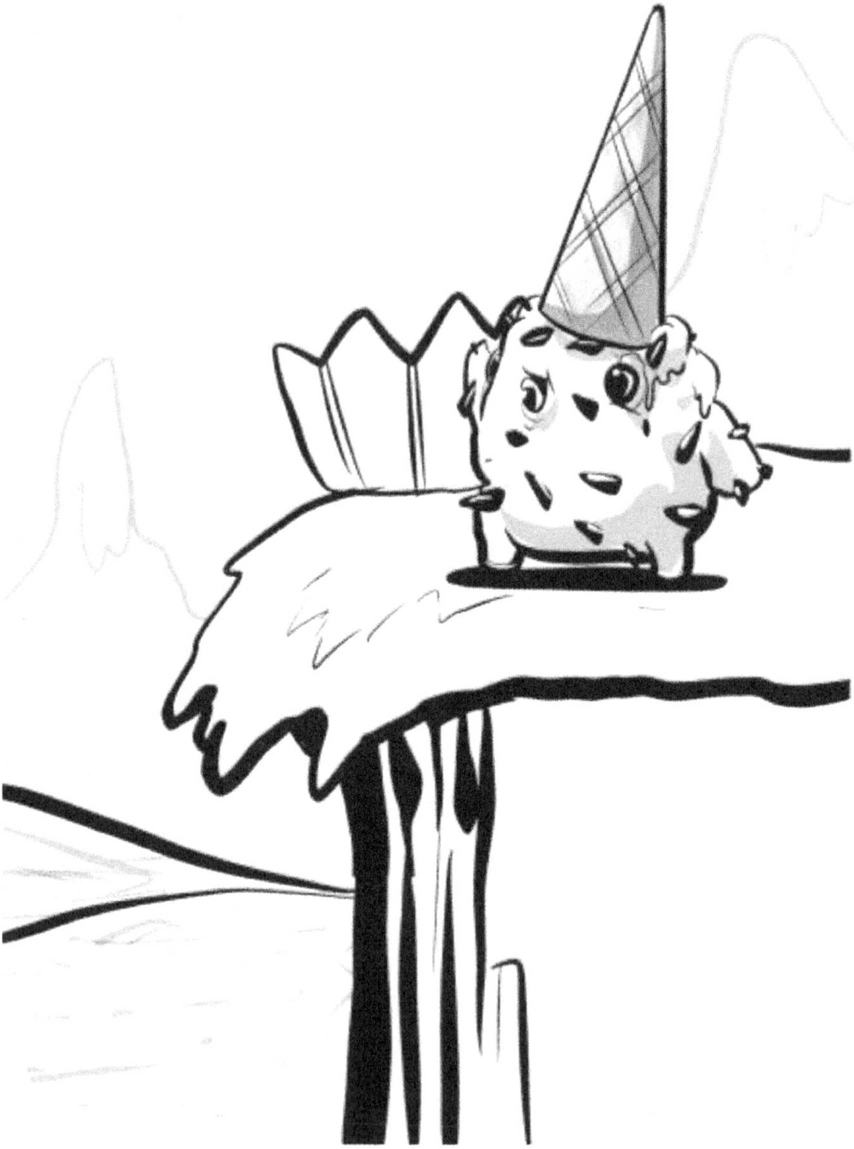

Lying on his back, Todd looked to the blue sky as he gently swirled down in the oversized cupcake wrapper and landed in a field of sprinkles. Just being around such a heap of them made Todd's teeth hurt.

One after the other, everyone floated down and gathered beneath a weeping willow with leaves of sour strings. Jen had been quiet since she saw that photo of Grandpa with the rainbow gem. She looked to Candy Mountain and couldn't keep her curiosity in any longer.

"You had it Arthur, the rainbow gem…Where is it now?" she asked out of the blue.

"What are you talking about now?" Grandpa asked.

"I saw the picture at the museum…Do you not remember because we can go back," Jen replied and took out her wand of time.

Anastasia snatched the wand before anything bad happened.

"What are you doing? Have these gems changed you or have you always been this ridiculous?" Anastasia asked.

"Always ridiculous…" Grandpa snickered.

After a receiving nothing more from Jen than a long pause, Anastasia whipped the wand into the Caramel River—It was so thick nothing was to be found in there. Everyone watched as Jen jumped in after the wand in a panic.

"You don't understand! You've never seen what they can do!" Jen said.

"We have and it's always been trouble, Mom," Anastasia said.

"When all hope is lost those gems give you some," Jen stopped as her knees sunk into the caramel.

"There's more to life than the treasure at the end of the hunt Jen, why do you think we're all here," Grandpa said.

"Who you've got to help you get by is all the hope you need," Todd added.

"I'm sorry," Jen sniffed and struggled to crawl out of the thick caramel.

"After a lot of searching, we found you, and I'd like to keep it that way," Anastasia said.

"Thank you…" Jen gave her a hug, and in a way, she felt a little relieved that the wand was gone.

7.

Slushie slopes

"Alright...Now, get bundled up. Where about to trek through the Slushie Slopes," Grandpa pulled on a hat.
    The closer they came to the slopes the frostier the candy grass became and eventually it started to snow—the slushie kind.
    "Ugh, it's so cold and wet," Anastasia complained.
    "Two words...Pon...Cho," Grandpa said and whipped out a five-pack of plastic ponchos hoping they would keep them dry.
    Todd squinted through the gloom and while reading the map estimated they were a bit off track near an abandoned ski resort.
    Poof!
    Todd ran into a lump of snow...A growling lump of snow. Flint hid between Anastasia's boots and she knew that meant trouble. A brawny snowman snarled showing his rotted candy teeth, he was carrying a tied-up candy cane deer over his shoulder.

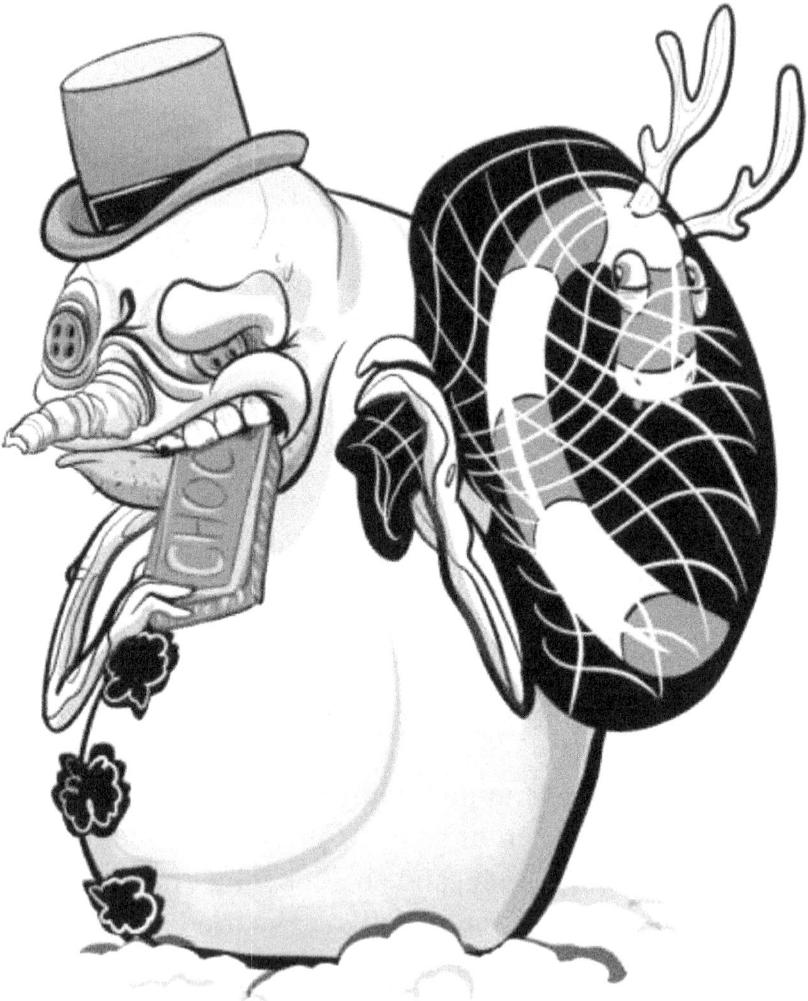
CHOC

"Uh...W...What are you gonna do with that candy cane deer?" Todd stuttered with eyes fixed on the snowman's broken carrot nose.

"I don't ask you what you do with your food...Do I?" the monstrous snowman asked and shuffled away while the candy cane deer cried.

"Boy, this is one of those situations I advise you to let go," Grandpa whispered. Anastasia looked at Todd with sad eyes.

"Grandpa, you actually always tell me to help..." Todd took a deep breath and left the others behind a boulder to sneak up on the snowman.

"Bet you wish I still had the wand now," Jen muttered.

While Todd crept behind the snowman, he sawed at the net with a knife from his keychain until the candy deer fell free and scurried off to safety.

Feeling the weight off his back, the snowman halted and held up an empty net. The snowman let out a large roar and turned batting his wooden arms. Todd dodged the pointy thrusts and came racing back.

"Run!" Todd screamed and shoved everyone along towards the abandoned ski resort.

Jen took out her red gem and shot laser blasts at the snowman, but whatever melted off, the snowman instantly repaired with more snow, it was useless.

"The doors locked!" Todd jiggled the handle to the resort entrance.

Anastasia tried the ski lift. She turned the rusty key and gave it a kick to start.

Put…Put…

Grandpa came along and with a boost of adrenaline he leapt off his scooter while it was still moving and jumped onto the lift seat.

"Go! Go! Go!" Jen hopped in the last seat just as the snowman reached them.

As each chair chugged up Slushie Slope the sky turned a darker shade of slate grey and the falling snow thickened. Jen heard a noise and turned to see the snowman shimmying towards them using the ski chairs like monkey bars. She took out her red gem again and aimed to blast, but this time, the laser accidentally hit the ski lifts chain system and brought everyone to a creaking halt.

"What happened?" Anastasia looked back and saw the snowman right behind them.

"I don't know but we're not far from the top and I'd like to get back down as soon as possible," Todd said feeling a drastic drop in temperature.

"It's either we get pushed or push on, and I'd rather take my chances," Grandpa said. He fell from the chair and landed face first in the deep snow.

Standing at the mountain peak, the wind chilled everyone to the bone, Flint was nearly a popsicle and the snowman was angrier than ever.

"We need to act fast," Anastasia shivered and could barely move his fingers.

"Taffy sleds," Grandpa kicked at a taffy tree stump.

Todd helped break off enough pieces of frozen taffy and sent everyone down the slope.

"Raaaaa!" the snowman came up behind Todd and grabbed him by the backpack.

"Ahhhhhhh!" Todd struck the snowman with the taffy and hopped on down the slope.

Gaining serious speed, Todd dodged candy rocks, hit small snowy jumps, and prepared for the bottom which was coming fast.

Thud

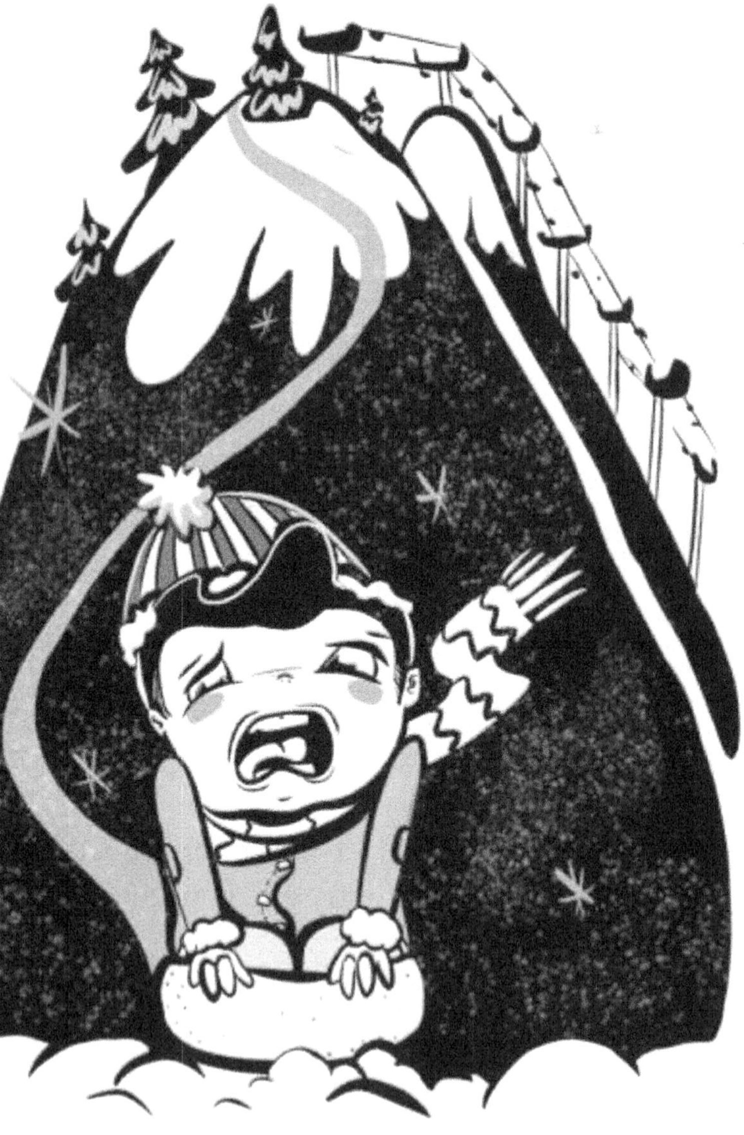

Todd hit a hidden rock and was launched through a pile of fluffy snow. He landed spinning across a frozen pond where small penguins were ice skating.

"Huh..."

Someone grabbed Todd and slid him to the side of the pond.

"Shh...They want us to sit and watch," Anastasia whispered.

A penguin ran by and covered Todd with a cotton candy blanket. Quiet music started playing and lights flashed from behind the pine trees. Six penguins skated out in a line and got ready to perform a dance on the ice. Stacking up high and shimmying in sequences the penguins put on quite a show. Flint was so excited that he slipped out of Anastasia's lap and drifted out in the center of the frozen pond. He tried to scurry away as the penguins skated his way, but his little legs only jumbled in place.

Crash!

One after the other, the penguins tripped and fell into a pile. The music cut out and the penguins began to yell and chitter, but no one could understand a thing they were saying. Anastasia slowly clapped as Flint jumped into her coat.

Bickering up a storm, the penguins shoved everyone off the ice and back onto the path. One penguin held up a fist before returning to the ice to skate again. Grandpa was panting from only walking ten feet.

"What about your scooter?" Todd asked.

"Scoot-shmoot...Good thing it wasn't a rental. I can get around the old-fashioned way..." Grandpa said and snatched a candy cane from the ground to use and a walking stick.

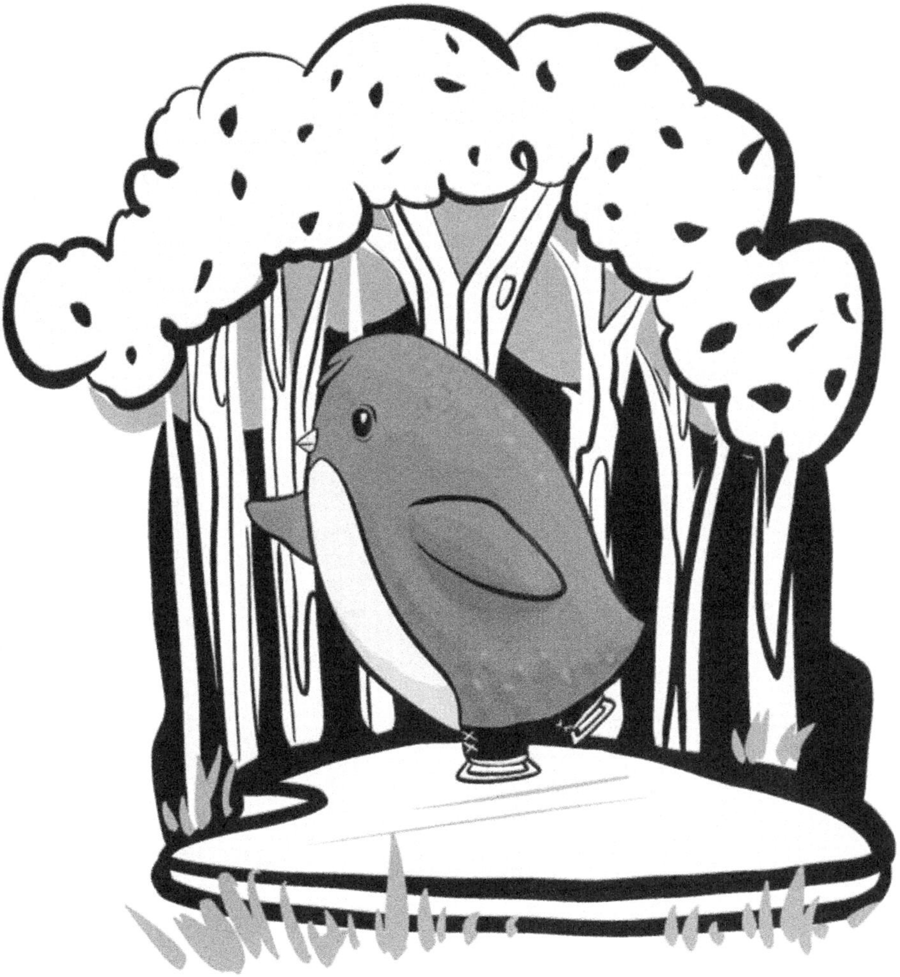

8.

Candy Thieves

"There used to be a forest here," Grandpa said as they walked into a stump-filled field—It had been cleaned out, but by what?

"Be careful! Bad snowmen are cutting down candy trees!" a passing raccoon said.

"Shhh..." said Jen.

The sound of a large running engine hummed through their ears.

Anastasia peeked from behind a bush and saw five snowmen with saws clearing away trees and capturing candies. It looked to be a makeshift station area with a rocket, crates and cages.

"Oh my gosh, there he is again!" Anastasia gasped and pointed to the snowman with the broken carrot nose that had chased them before.

"Oh, that's it...Hey you! You better cut that out!" Todd stepped out from behind the bush. As scared as he was, seeing the poor candies made him speak before thinking.

"Quiet boy!" Grandpa smacked Todd in the side with his cane.

"That's what we is doin—Cuttin'…What's it to ya?" a tall snowman said and cracked a branch in half.

"You, again! You're lucky you're not made a candy, or you'd all be gone by now," the snowman with the broken nose lifted Todd off the ground, licked his cheek and threw him aside.

"Yuck…"

"I can tell the temperature has dropped here due to the coldness of your heart," Grandpa said and helped Todd up.

"Sidown, fossil," the snowman knocked Grandpa over with a snowball.

"Since yous like to keep pokin' your fleshy nose in other people's business we'll let you sit here and watch a while," the tall snowman said and pulled a lever that caged everyone in a black licorice trap.

"There ain't gonna be no little candy deers tryin to save you now is there!" the snowman laughed and loaded bunches of bags into their spaceship.

Todd grew sick watching all the candy be taken and destroyed, and there was nothing he could do.

The spaceship door closed, and the snowmen thieves blasted off towards the sky. They had gotten away with everything.

"Hope you all are hungry, that's going to be our only way out of here," Grandpa said and began to bite at the licorice cage.

"Come on Flint, help me," Anastasia said, but Flint was not having any part of it, he was busy jumping after a peppermint bird hopping outside the trap.

"These taste awful," Jen bit a chunk of thick licorice and spit it out.

Todd got out his keychain knife and began poking at the licorice, but it was so strong the knife snapped in two.

"Stupid snowman..." Todd looked up at the sky from within the cage.

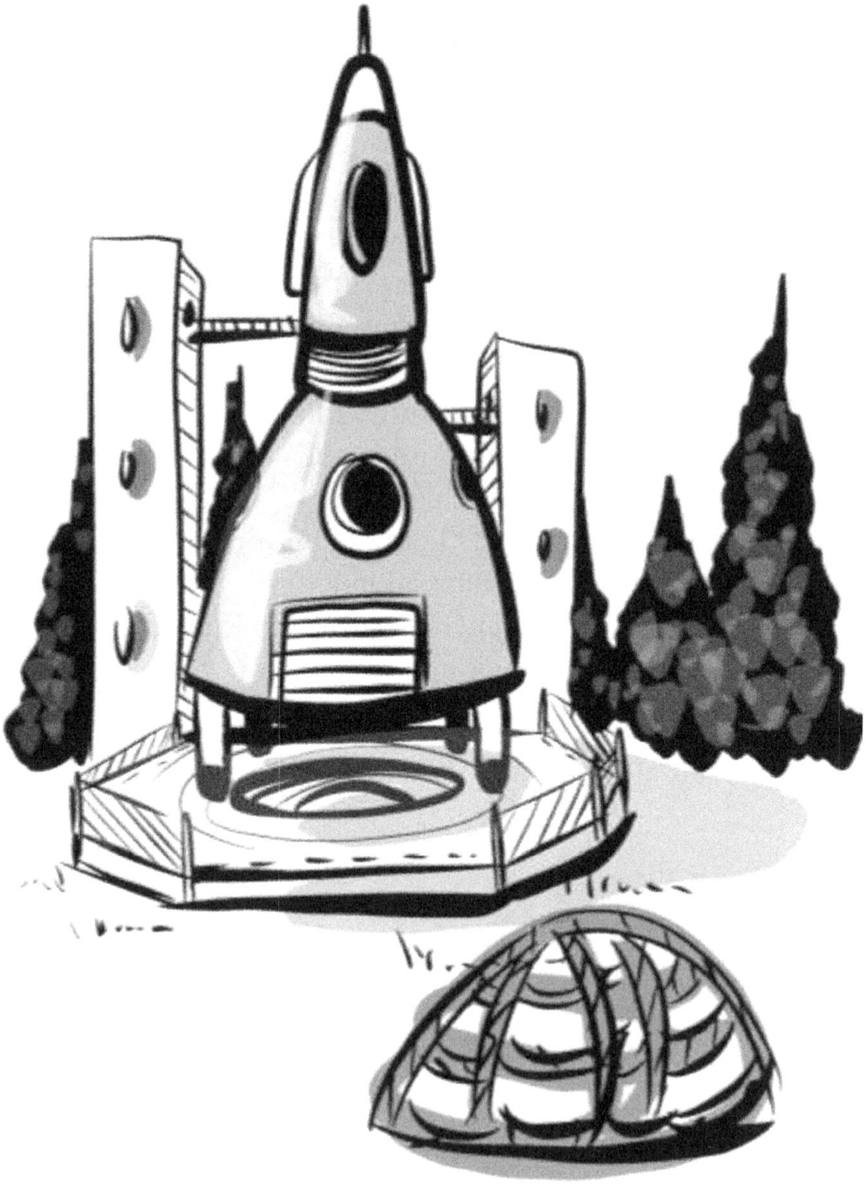

With blackened tongues everyone was finally free but seeing the aftermath of what the thieving snowmen had done made Todd's stomach welt with disgust.

"You want to get them back, don't you?" Jen asked.

"Yep..." Todd replied.

"We may not be able to blast the snowmen with this gem but blasting their form of transportation should keep some peace around here for a little while, don't you think," Jen said and placed the red gem in Todd's hand.

Todd smiled and walked over to the landing platform with a plan.

"You're going to leave it sit there? What's that going to do?" Anastasia asked.

"I rigged the gem to the platform so that when anything lands on this baby it'll be blown straight back where it came from," Todd said wiping frosting from his hands.

"Good work," Jen said proud.

"Better hope it goes that way...Looks like the Sweet Sanctuary is just around the corner then we'll get to finally relax a little," Grandpa said and read the map.

Back on track, the mountains shrunk behind them as they followed the sun. Todd and Anastasia hung back while Grandpa and Jen talked. They seemed to be getting along better now.

"All I have to say is our legs are gonna be chiseled from all this walking," Todd looked back at his calves. Anastasia giggled.

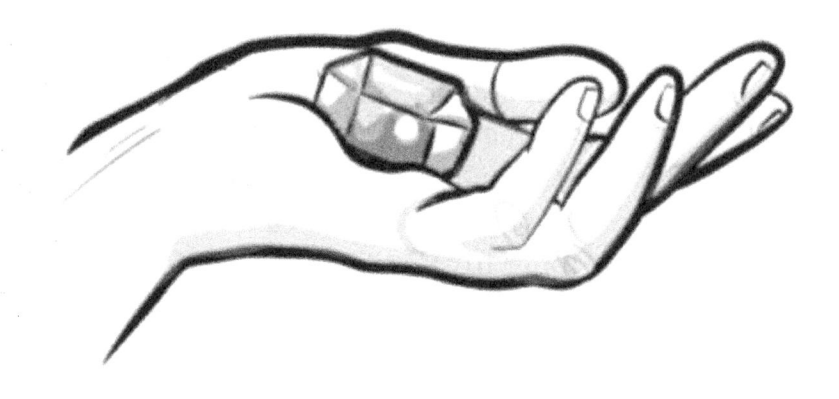

9.

Sweet Sanctuary

  Bubblegum birds chirped between the clouds as the dirt path dispersed into a sweet-smelling meadow of marshmallow flowers.
  "Now what's this? Wasn't here before..." Grandpa knocked on the tall white fence with his cane. It seemed to stretch a mile each way with no sign of entry.
  Anastasia climbed up the fence and peeked over.
  "Why hi..." said a cyclops.
  "Is there a door to get in around here?" Anastasia asked.
  The cyclops walked over and ripped a whole set of planks clean off the fence.
  "That'll do," Grandpa said. He shuffled through to the other side of the fence and knew right away that they were in the sanctuary. Delightful ponds bordered the bumpy South and small candy animals filled the wide-open fields.

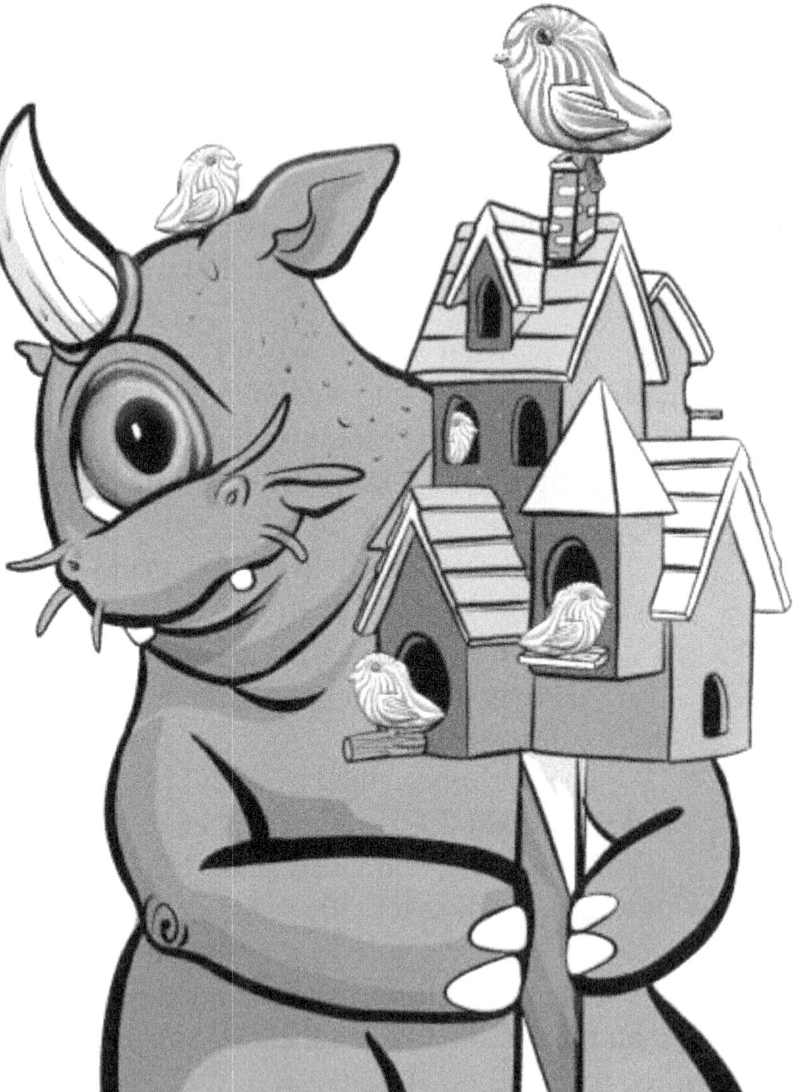

"Names Bo...You all seem like some nice folks," the cyclops said and put the fence back while covered in peppermint birds.

"This is some house," Todd said admiring detail in the peppermint bird house. It was even was furnished with mini couches.

"Oh, yes, these creatures are special. Without them the candy forests wouldn't grow. They're very smart and tend to stick around those they like," Bo said.

"Is Ben still here?" Grandpa asked.

"Ah, Ben...Unfortunately no, he disappeared in a sugar storm...So, thank goodness Yumi's taken over or else half these creatures would be extinct by now...We've got some bad snowmen on the loose," Bo explained.

"Oh, we know all about those," Todd said and had two peppermint birds land on his head.

Bo took everyone over to the storage shed to feed the chocolate bears and gum bunnies. Anastasia poured Flint a cup of dog food while Grandpa sprinkled gummy leaves around the hopping gum bunnies.

"Oh, hey everyone," Yumi passed by and lowered a five-foot candy fish into the pond.

"The peppermint birds said you've had an eventful time getting here," Yumi told them.

"You can talk to birds?" Anastasia asked.

"Mhm...And one of them brought back this wand of yours too," Yumi pulled the wand of time from her pocket.

"What..." Jen said shocked. She thought it'd be gone forever.

"Thank you..." Jen said after Yumi handed it to her.

"I haven't seen you since you were a baby, but I can tell you have your father's eyes," Grandpa told Yumi.

"I've heard your stories, Arthur. You've done a lot for this island," Yumi smiled.

"If you're headed to the hotel, Bo can show you to the rear gate near the farm, but feel free to stop back any time," Yumi said.

"The candies always love company, and they'll keep you busy for hours," Bo said and picked up a baby snow cone.

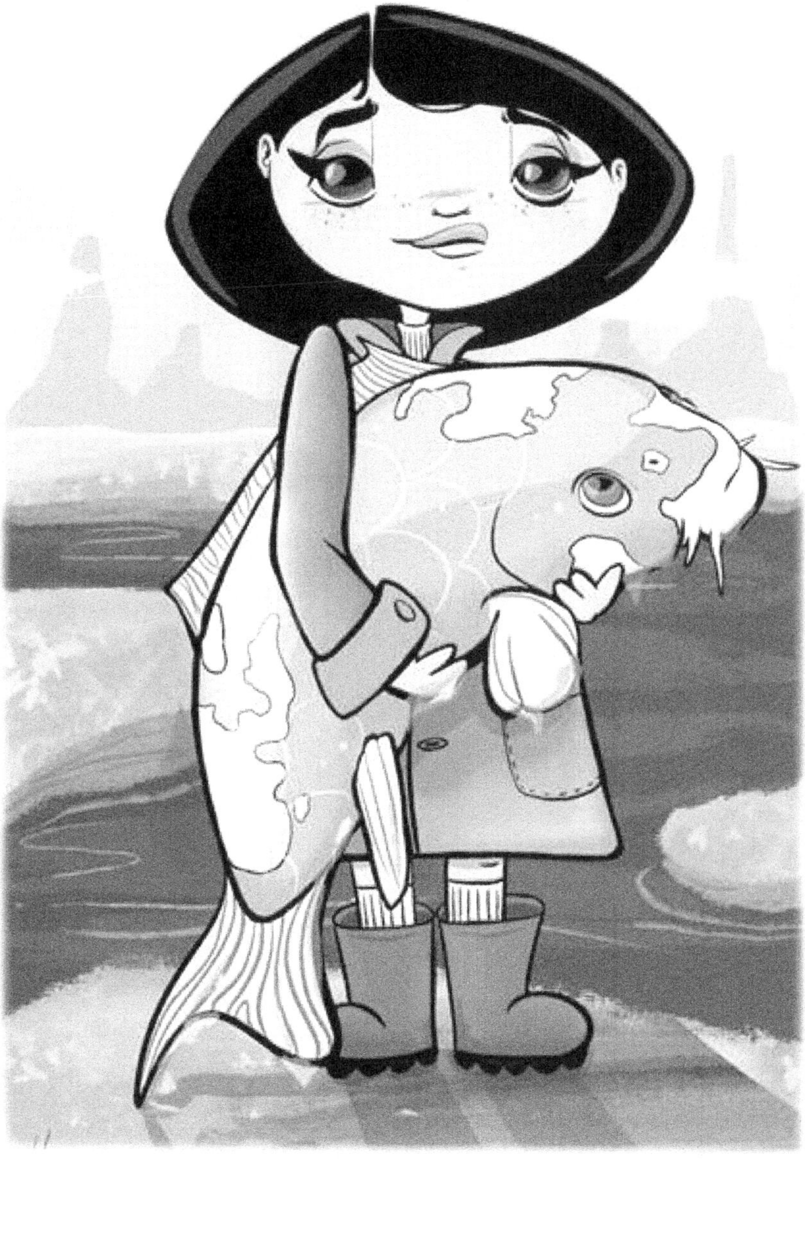

10.

Honey Hotel

After saying farewell to the sanctuary, they followed hexagon tiles, and just passed a garden of berry bushes there it was.

"Here's the old hive…Hope none of you are allergic to bees…Just kidding," Grandpa joked and opened the door.

Ding

"Hey! Arthur! Nice to see you again!" the desk candy said.

"I used to work here at the hotel for a short time…Was in charge of the honeycomb vault," Grandpa whispered to Todd.

"If you'll be staying a few days, how does hive one sound?" the desk candy asked and placed a key on the counter.

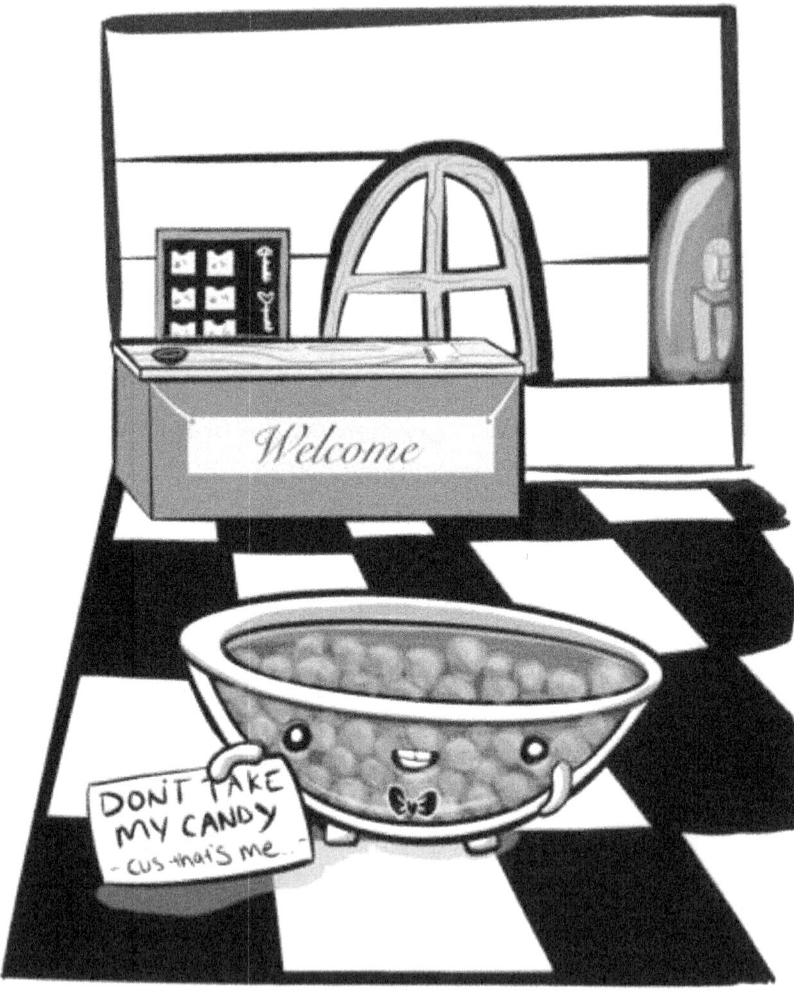
Welcome
DON'T TAKE
MY CANDY
-CUS that's me...-

"That's always been my favorite," Grandpa replied.

Over to the side, Jen noticed an encased gem framed on the wall. It was the rainbow gem, the one that could make sweet dreams come true. Stuck in a trance she walked closer.

"That there's the legendary rainbow gem mined by Arthur himself, actually. It's quite the attraction and keeps business booming here at the hotel," the desk candy said.

Jen looked at Grandpa, stumped as to why he never used it.

"Yep, the gems belong to the islands," Grandpa said and glared back at Jen who smiled softly.

On the way to their rooms, Todd saw the golden honey vault and all the busy bees working in the hive halls.

"This place always feels a little like home," Grandpa said and unlocked the hexagon door to their room.

"Room service!" a yellow candy said and danced in dusting.

"Here's your souvenir. Thanks for staying with us!" the candy handed him a chest and danced out dusting.

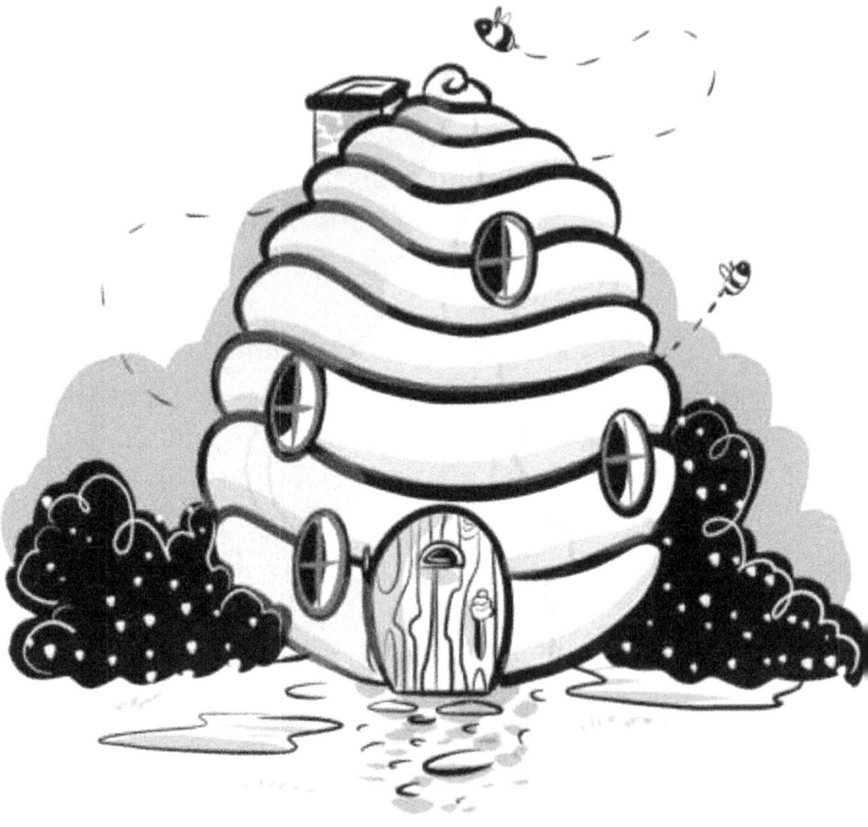

"Now, this is the kind of treasure that's worth the walk…Go on and take as much as you want," Grandpa grabbed a handful of coins and passed the treasure box to Anastasia.

"Chocolateoons…" Grandpa unwrapped the gold covered chocolate coin and winked at Todd.

Boom!

A huge explosion went off in the distance. Everyone ran to the window.

"Got 'em…" Jen said referring to the trap he had left for the snowmen.

Todd smiled.

Knock-Knock

"I forgot, here's your receipt," the desk candy said and handed Todd an envelope from the door.

"Go on Todd, it's for you," Grandpa sat back.

Todd opened the envelope and read what appeared to be a receipt for one candy boat.

"What?" Todd questioned.

"Back at the Milkshake Museum, Rory mentioned he knew some local workers, so I traded him a rare and valuable candy in exchange for a new boat," Grandpa explained.

"Wow, but how is candy going to float?" Todd asked.

"Boy, it's carved from the finest jawbreakers and epoxy coated. One of a kind, it'll hold don't worry…So get your sea legs back in shape, you'll be taking us home," Grandpa said and tossed Todd a coin.

Look out for more Odd Lands books!

Available on Amazon and other sites.

—Odd Lands Collection 1-4—

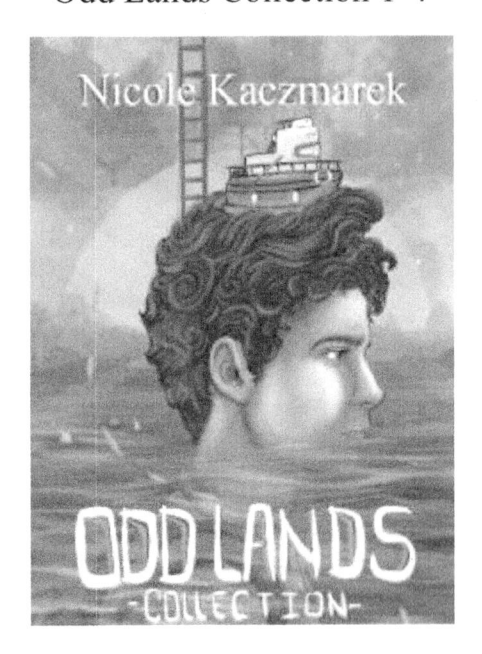

Or sold individually:

Book one: An Adventure to Remember
Book two: The Burning Desert
Book three: The Depths
Book four: Above the Clouds
Book five: A Sweet Getaway

Made in the USA
Monee, IL
03 November 2021